The Tale of Old Dog Spot

Arthur Scott Bailey

THE TALE OF OLD DOG SPOT

I

ALMOST TWINS

Nobody ever spoke of old Spot's master as "old Johnnie Green." Yet the two—boy and dog—were almost exactly the same age. Somehow Spot grew up faster than Johnnie. He had stopped being a puppy by the time his young master learned to walk. And when Johnnie was big enough to play around the farm buildings his parents felt sure that he was safe so long as "old Spot," as they called the dog, was with him.

Spot thought himself years older than the small boy; or at least he always acted so. If a goose hissed at little, toddling Johnnie Green, old Spot would drive the goose away, barking in a loud voice, "Don't you frighten this child!" If Johnnie went into the stable and wandered within reach of the horses' heels Spot would take hold of his clothes and draw him gently back out of danger. And if Johnnie strayed to the duck pond the old dog wouldn't leave him even to chase the cat, but stayed right there by the pond, ready to pull his young charge out of the water in case he happened to fall in.

Spot seemed to enjoy his task of taking care of Johnnie Green. It wasn't all work. A great deal of pleasure went with his duties, for Johnnie Green never wanted to do anything but play. And Spot wasn't so grown up that he couldn't enjoy a lively romp. For that matter, he never did get over his liking for boisterous fun.

Still, there were some kinds of sport that he didn't care for. He wasn't fond of having such things as tin cans tied to his tail. He disliked to be harnessed to a toy wagon. He hated to have his ears pulled. Yet there was only one offense that ever made him growl. When Johnnie Green took a bone away from him Spot couldn't help warning him, with a deep, rumbling grumbling, that he was going too far, even between friends. But he never snapped at Johnnie. That growling was only Spot's way of teaching Johnnie Green manners.

Fond as he was of his young master, Spot did not care to spend all his time playing childish games. There were grown-up things that he liked to do — things in which a toddler like Johnnie Green couldn't take part. Around the farmhouse there were always the cat to be teased and squirrels to be chased into trees. In the pasture there were woodchucks to be hunted; and even if he couldn't catch them it was fun to see those fat fellows tumble into their holes.

Then there were the cows. Spot loved to help Farmer Green drive them home late in the afternoon. He acted very important when he went for the cows, always pretending that it was hard work, though he really thought it great sport.

Sometimes when Johnnie Green wanted to play with Spot the old dog couldn't be found anywhere. He might be over the hill, visiting a neighbor's dog. He might be in the woods, looking for birds. He might even have followed a wagon to the village.

As Johnnie Green grew older he roamed through the woods with Spot. And when Johnnie's father at last let him own a gun, old Spot was as pleased as Johnnie was.

"I've been waiting for this event for several years," Spot told the Muley Cow.

She did not share his delight.

"For pity's sake, keep that boy and his gun out of the pasture!" she bellowed. "It frightens me to have him come near me with his blunderbuss."

Old Spot gave her a pitying look.

"It's plain," he said, "that you don't come from a sporting family, as I do, or you'd never speak in that fashion of a nice new shotgun. You know I'm a sporting dog. I'm a pointer. I point out the game for the hunters."

The Muley Cow gave a sort of snort and tossed her head.

"It's lucky for Johnnie Green," she sniffed, "that I'm not a sporting cow, or he might not have any butter on his bread."

II
TEASING THE CAT

When Miss Kitty Cat came to the farmhouse to live she soon showed old dog Spot that she could fight like a vixen. The first time he cornered her she put some scratches on his nose that he never forgot. And after that he always took great pains to keep out of reach of Miss Kitty's claws.

So long as Miss Kitty Cat ran away from him Spot would follow her, yelping madly. But when she stopped, he stopped too, digging his own claws into the dirt in order to leave a safe distance between Miss Kitty and his nose.

He quickly discovered that there were ways in which he could tease Miss Kitty Cat that annoyed her greatly, while keeping his nose out of harm's way. Growling always made her tail grow big. Barking made her spit at him. But there was something else that angered her still more. When Spot stood stock still one day, with his tail stuck straight out behind him, and pointed at her with his nose, he made her almost frantic.

"What are you pointing at with that long nose of yours?" Miss Kitty Cat snarled.

Spot didn't say a word. For the moment he didn't move any more than the iron dog did, that stood in a yard on the outskirts of the village and never so much as wagged his tail from one year's end to another.

Somehow Spot's queer behavior gave Miss Kitty Cat an odd, creepy feeling along her back. Her fur rose on end. She glared at Spot and spat at him in a most unladylike fashion.

Spot found it very hard to stand still and never let out a single yelp. Once he almost whined. But he managed to stifle the sound.

"If she swells up much more she's likely to burst," he thought.

"Go away!" Miss Kitty scolded. "Don't you know better than to stare at a lady?"

5

Never an answer did old Spot make.

It was a little more than Miss Kitty Cat could endure. With a yowl that had in it something of anger and something of fear, too, she jumped off the doorstep where she had been sitting and whisked around the corner of the house.

With Miss Kitty's first leap Spot came suddenly to life. He barked joyfully and followed her. Miss Kitty Cat ran up a tree in the yard and stayed there until Spot went off chuckling.

"I'm glad I played that trick on her," he said to himself. "It seems to bother her more than anything else I've ever tried."

Thereafter Spot often pointed at Miss Kitty when he met her, either inside the house or about the yard. And she never failed to fly into a passion.

"Such manners I never saw!" she spluttered when she talked one day with a cat from the nearest farmhouse.

"I'd soon cure the old dog of that unpleasant trick if he tried it on me," her neighbor remarked.

"What would you do?" Miss Kitty Cat wanted to know.

"I'd chase him."

"He can run faster than I can," said Miss Kitty.

"When he's pointing at you, jump at him before he can turn around. If you drag your claws across his nose just once he'll be careful after that to look the other way when he sees you."

"Your plan sounds as if it might be worth trying," said Miss Kitty thoughtfully.

III

A WILD DOG

Old dog Spot felt greatly pleased with himself. He had told everybody that would listen to him how he could make Miss Kitty Cat angry just by standing still and pointing at her.

"You'd better leave that cat alone," the old horse Ebenezer advised him. "Don't you remember how she clawed you when you cornered her in this barn one day?"

"I remember—yes!" Spot admitted, as he looked cross-eyed at his nose, which still bore the marks of Miss Kitty's claws. "I'm careful not to stand too near her," he explained. "I don't try to grab her. I just stare at her. And she gets wild."

"A wild cat," old Ebenezer warned him, "is a dangerous creature."

"Nonsense!" said Spot. "She always sneaks away after I've pointed at her for a few minutes. It's the funniest sight! If you could see it once you'd know she was terribly afraid of me."

"Nonsense!" said the old horse Ebenezer. But he couldn't make Spot believe there was the slightest danger in teasing Miss Kitty Cat.

"She always runs up a tree after I've been pointing at her," Spot went on.

"You'd better look out!" Ebenezer cautioned him. "She'll have you climbing a tree the first thing you know."

Well, that made Spot laugh. And he went out of the barn feeling even more pleased with himself than ever. He was sorry that Miss Kitty Cat wasn't in the yard. He felt just like bothering her.

"I'll go up to the pasture and find me a woodchuck to chase," Spot said to himself, for he was in such high spirits that he simply had to have fun of some sort.

First, however, he decided to stop and dig up a bone that he had buried in the flower garden. So he trotted across the yard. And as he drew near the farmhouse he changed his plans all at once. He forgot his bone and he forgot his woodchuck, too. For he caught sight of something that had escaped his eye before. Stretched on the ledge outside one of the kitchen windows Miss Kitty Cat was enjoying a nap in the sunshine.

"Aha!" said Spot very softly. "Aha! Here's a bit of luck." And he turned sharply aside and hurried towards the house, to come to a dead stop beneath the window and stand there motionless with his nose pointing at the sleeping form of Miss Kitty.

Though Spot didn't make the slightest noise the sleeper suddenly opened her eyes.

"Tchah!" she exclaimed, springing to her feet and glaring at her annoyer.

Spot Bolted Through the Barn Door.

(Page 16)

If the window hadn't been closed no doubt Miss Kitty would have slipped through it into the kitchen. But there was no escape that way.

"It's a pity," she muttered, "that a person can't take a cat nap without being stared at by this old dog. I think it's about time I took my neighbor's advice and taught him to keep his eyes and his nose where they belong."

Then Miss Kitty Cat jumped. She jumped off the window ledge straight at old dog Spot, who was still gazing up at her from below.

When he saw her coming he gave a startled yelp and tried to dodge her. But he was too slow. Miss Kitty Cat landed squarely on his back and clawed him savagely.

Old Spot dashed half way across the farmyard, then dropped suddenly and rolled over and over on the ground.

The next instant he was on his feet again and tearing toward the barn. Though Miss Kitty had dropped off his back and was already on her way to the house he did not look around to see what had become of her.

Spot bolted through the barn door and scurried into an empty stall, where he jumped into the manger and cowered down in the hay that half filled it, and moaned.

It was the stall next to the old horse Ebenezer's. And that mild fellow peered over at him in wonder. "What has happened?" he inquired.

"The cat scratched me," Spot told him. "I was teasing her and she wasn't at all nice about it."

"What were you doing — pointing at her?" Ebenezer asked him.

"Yes!"

"I suppose it made her wild," the old horse remarked. "And a wild cat is a dangerous creature."

Spot whined fretfully. He wished he could lick his wounds. But how can one lick scratches when they are behind one's ears?

"I was a wild dog for a few moments," he groaned. "I never dreamed she would plump down on me like that."

"Haven't you ever heard of it's raining cats and dogs?" Ebenezer said. "Well, to-day it rained cats."

IV

THE WOODPILE

Farmer Green always had a woodpile in the back yard. Sometimes it was big. Sometimes it was little. Sometimes it was mostly made up of four-foot logs. Sometimes the logs were all split and sawed, ready to burn.

When Farmer Green and the hired man had nothing more pressing to do they set to work on the woodpile. It was surprising how fast the big sticks grew into firewood under their axes and saws.

One day they started sawing and splitting when Johnnie Green and old dog Spot were roaming through the woods. And when Johnnie and Spot came back home, just in time for dinner, they found a great heap of firewood lying on the ground where there had been nothing but dirt when they started for the woods some hours before.

Old dog Spot ran straight to the woodpile and began sniffing and scratching and whining.

If Johnnie Green hadn't been hungry he would have paid more heed to Spot's behavior. But the men had already gone into the house. And Johnnie hurried after them, leaving Spot to nose about the woodpile as he pleased.

"Humph!" Spot growled. "Seems to me Johnnie Green might stay here a while and help me. I've been chasing woodchucks and squirrels for him all the morning. And I showed him a few birds, too."

Spot never once left the woodpile while Johnnie was eating his dinner. When Johnnie and his father and the hired man came out of the house later old Spot began to yelp. He made frantic efforts to burrow down beneath the pile of firewood, stopping now and then to run up to his young master and bark.

Now that he had had his dinner, Johnnie Green was all ready for any sort of fun.

"Spot smells some kind of game in the woodpile!" Johnnie exclaimed.

"Perhaps he does," said his father. "But I don't see how he's going to get hold of it unless we move the woodpile. And I don't believe we'll quit work to help the old dog catch a chipmunk — or maybe a rat."

"Come on!" Spot begged Johnnie, as plainly as he could bark. "Move some of this wood for me! There's something under it that I want to get my teeth on."

"All right! All right!" Johnnie told him. And to his father Johnnie said, "Do you care if I throw some of the stove wood over on the other side of the pile?"

"If you're going to move any wood —" Farmer Green replied with a wink at the hired man — "if you're going to move any wood you might as well move it into the woodshed and pile it up neatly."

When he heard that suggestion Johnnie Green looked very glum. For a minute or two he thought he wouldn't bother to help old Spot find what he was looking for. But Spot teased and teased. And Johnnie couldn't help being curious to know what it was that Spot was after.

"Maybe there's a muskrat here," he said to himself. "If there is, I'll have his skin to pay me for my trouble."

V

A DEEP SECRET

Old Spot wouldn't let Johnnie Green alone. He kept jumping against him and whining, begging him to move some of the wood, because there was something very, very interesting beneath it.

Still Johnnie hesitated. He hadn't intended to do any work that afternoon.

"After all," he thought, "I'll have to help carry in this wood sooner or later. Really, I might as well take some of it into the woodshed now."

To Spot's delight he bent over and began gathering an armful of wood.

"Wow! Wow!" Spot howled. "Thank goodness I'm going to get what's under this pile, after all."

Johnnie Green carried armful after armful of wood from the yard and piled it in the shed back of the kitchen. All the time old dog Spot was urging him with yelps and barks and whines and moans to move faster. And all the time Johnnie Green was working as spryly as he could.

Whatever it might be that Spot wanted to get under the woodpile in the yard, Johnnie hoped it wouldn't escape through the crevices between the sticks.

"I don't want to get myself all tired out for nothing," Johnnie said to himself. "I was going fishing this afternoon."

While Johnnie hurried back and forth between the woodpile and the shed Spot clawed away at the edge of the pile. He thrust his nose beneath loose sticks and pushed them about. He uttered pitiful sounds.

"I never saw that dog take on so," Farmer Green remarked.

"And I never saw Johnnie work so hard," said the hired man. "When there's wood to be carried in he's usually a mile away."

Farmer Green laughed.

12

"He'll quit as soon as Spot gets what he wants," he replied. "It's too bad this sort of thing doesn't happen oftener. Except for driving the cows home, this is the first time I ever knew a boy and a dog to do much besides play, when they're together."

Turkey Proudfoot, the huge gobbler, came hurrying around the corner of the barn to see what was going on. He had an idea that he ruled the farmyard.

"What's all this row about?" he gobbled at old Spot. "Have you lost something?"

"Yes!" Spot told him. "Johnnie Green's helping me to find it. We're moving part of the woodpile."

"What did you lose?" Turkey Proudfoot demanded.

Old Spot pretended not to hear him. He began barking again at Johnnie Green.

Mr. Catbird, who loved to play jokes on everybody, started mewing from his hiding place under the lilac bushes. He had noticed Spot's antics. And he hoped to fool him into thinking there was a strange cat around the place. For Spot was a famous chaser of all cats—so long as they kept running away from him and didn't turn around and try to scratch him.

To Mr. Catbird's astonishment old Spot paid no heed to his catcalls.

"This is queer," Mr. Catbird muttered. "Whenever I've mewed before he has always come a-running. There must be something uncommonly interesting under that woodpile."

VI
BURIED TREASURE

Henrietta Hen, who was one of the busiest busybodies on the farm, came along and stood and watched old dog Spot while he dug and scratched and howled about the woodpile.

"What on earth is the matter with you?" she asked him. "I don't make half that fuss when I've just laid an egg and really have something to cackle about."

"I've no time to talk with you now," Spot told Henrietta Hen. "Can't you see that Johnnie Green and I are moving the woodpile?"

"Why are you doing that?" Henrietta inquired.

"There's something beneath it that I want," he said hurriedly.

Henrietta Hen gave a sudden start.

"I wonder if it's a weasel!" she exclaimed. And since he didn't reply, and she had learned to be mortally afraid of weasels, she ran off squawking, to hide high up in the haymow in the barn.

Johnnie Green hadn't carried away much more of the woodpile when old dog Spot began to dig furiously in the dirt. And in a few seconds' time he unearthed a big bone.

It was a choice bone. He had buried it several days before. And when he came back from the woods and found a woodpile on top of the place where he had hidden it, it was no wonder that he made such a howdy-do.

Johnnie Green looked much upset as he stood stock still and saw Spot trot away with the bone in his mouth.

"So that was what he was after all the time!" he cried at last. "I hoped it was a muskrat."

His father and the hired man laughed and laughed.

"I don't see any joke," Johnnie grumbled. "Here I've piled up wood enough in the shed to last a month. And I might have been fishing all the time."

"Well," said his father, "whose fault is it?"

"Old Spot's, I should think!" Johnnie replied.

"I don't see how you can blame him," said Farmer Green. "Suppose you had buried a piece of strawberry shortcake here, expecting to eat it for your dinner. And suppose there wasn't another piece as good — or as big — to be had anywhere. And suppose you had come back from a tramp in the woods, hungry as — well, hungry as you were this noon. Wouldn't you want that piece of shortcake? If you could get old Spot to move the wood off it, wouldn't you be glad to have him do it?"

"Maybe!" Johnnie admitted. "Maybe! But Spot wasn't after a piece of strawberry shortcake. He was after an old bone. And he fooled me."

"I should say that you fooled yourself," his father retorted. "Anyhow, we're going to have strawberry shortcake for supper to-night. I heard your mother say so. And she made a special cake for you."

That news made Johnnie Green look a good deal less gloomy. In fact he almost smiled.

"I was going to give you that old fishing rod of mine if you'd help carry in the wood," Farmer Greene went on. "And you could take it now and go fishing, if you thought you could be home in time for supper."

"Hurrah!" Johnnie Green suddenly jumped up and down. "Hurrah!" he cried. "And thank you very much!"

And when, an hour later, old Spot came swimming across the creek and joined Johnnie on the further bank, and shook drops of water all over his young master, Johnnie Green only patted him and called him a "good old fellow."

VII

SWIMMING

Old dog Spot liked boys. Somehow they always managed to have a lively time; and usually they seemed glad to have him join them in their sports.

He never could understand why Johnnie Green and the neighbors' boys didn't want him to play baseball with them. Spot loved to chase a ball. And sometimes when he was watching a game and somebody hit a slow grounder he would rush out and grab the ball and run with it.

Then all the boys would run after him and try to catch him. That always pleased Spot mightily. And the longer the chase lasted the happier he was. But it was different with the boys. The harder they had to run after Spot before they got the ball away from him the more out of patience they became.

Whenever Spot took part in a ball game like that Johnnie Green usually put an end to his fun, for the time being, by tying him to something or other — perhaps a fence or a tree. But even that was better — so Spot thought — than being sent home in disgrace.

Luckily there were other sports in which Spot could romp with the boys as much as he pleased, without anybody's objecting. Nutting in the woods in the fall; skating on the mill pond or coasting down the long hill past Farmer Green's house in the winter; berrying in the summer — and swimming! Those were only a few of the jolly times that Spot and the boys enjoyed together.

Perhaps, of them all, both Spot and the boys liked swimming the most. As for Spot, he didn't care where he swam, so long as the water was wet. Broad Brook, Swift River, Black Creek, or the mill pond — any one of those places suited him as well as another. The boys, however, preferred the mill pond. It was deep enough, by the dam, to suit the best swimmers; and it was shallow enough at the upper end for those that were just learning.

All the boys thought it great fun when a wagon clattered over the bridge, which crossed right above the dam. Then they ducked into the water, with only their heads out, and shouted more or less politely at whoever was passing.

At such times Spot barked, because that seemed to him the gentlemanly thing to do. But he never could see any sense in jumping into the water if he happened to be out on the bank when a wagon came along.

The boys threw sticks about the pond for Spot to fetch back to them. They raced with him. They upset him when he was sunning himself on the big rock near the dam, and they laughed to see the splash he made when he struck the water.

No matter what tricks the boys played on him, Spot never lost his temper. He took everything good-naturedly. And one day, when Johnnie Green and his friends were swimming in the mill pond he even took a bundle of clothes from beneath a big hickory on the bank. Yes! Spot caught up somebody's clothes in his mouth and started along the road with them.

He was surprised to hear a terrible outcry from the water.

VIII

WHAT RED DID

Old dog Spot was trotting down the road from the mill pond, carrying a bundle of somebody's clothes in his mouth. When he heard frantic shouts from the water, where Johnnie Green and his friends were swimming, he quickened his pace.

One of the swimmers was known as "Red." And it was a favorite trick of his to tie hard knots in other boys' garments while the owners of them were in the pond. Usually he wet the knots, because wetting them made them harder to untie.

On this day somebody had turned the tables on Red. Somebody had crept up behind the big old hickory tree on the bank and had knotted Red's clothes tightly. That was why old Spot found a bundle under the tree, all tied up and ready to carry off.

It was no wonder that the boys began to yell when they saw Spot pick up those clothes and calmly trot away with them. It was no wonder that they swam to the bank and scrambled up to the big hickory to find out whose clothes were missing.

When they saw that Red was the unlucky one, everybody else began to whoop and laugh.

Spot Started After Frisky Squirrel.

(Page 42)

But not Red! He let out a frightened scream and started to follow old dog Spot.

To the great delight of his companions, the rattle of a wagon and the thud of a horse's feet sounded from up the road. And since some one must soon drive over the bridge, which crossed right above the dam, Red scurried back again and dived into the pond, into which Johnnie Green and the others had already plunged.

18

Red rose to the surface spluttering. And finding that he could touch bottom with his feet, he stood with his carroty head out of water, watching for the wagon.

It soon came into view, out of the woods, and the horse that drew it thundered upon the bridge. The horse was old Ebenezer; and Farmer Green was driving him.

"Hi!" Red shouted. "Stop! Wait a minute!"

Johnnie Green's father pulled Ebenezer to a halt.

"What's going on here?" he inquired.

"Spot took my clothes," Red explained. "He's run down the road with them. Get them for me — please!"

Hoots and catcalls from the other boys followed Red's speech, which was a wonderfully polite one — for him.

Farmer Green couldn't help laughing.

"I'm going to the village," he said. "If I find any clothes along the road I'll pick them up and put them in the wagon. And if you're here when I come back I'll give them to you."

"He'll be here!" Johnnie Green shouted. "Red'll wait for you."

"If you hurry, maybe you can catch Spot," Red called to Farmer Green as he drove off. "I can't stay here all day."

"You'll have to," the boys jeered.

"Maybe you'll have to wait here till dark," Johnnie Green suggested.

"I won't!" Red replied, as he swam towards the bank. "Your dog took my clothes," he cried as he ran up to the big hickory. "And I'm going to take yours."

It was Johnnie's turn to yell then. He was on the further side of the mill pond. And long before he could cross it Red had snatched up Johnnie's clothes from the shade of the hickory and dodged into the bushes with them.

IX

A BUNDLE OF CLOTHES

Old dog Spot was trotting down the road with the bundle of clothes in his mouth—the clothes which belonged to Johnnie Green's friend Red, who was one of the swimming party in the mill pond.

Somewhat to Spot's surprise the boys had not come tearing down the road after him.

"It's queer," he said to himself. "I wonder why they don't follow me. This would be fun if they'd only chase me."

Just then he happened to spy a squirrel on a stone wall. Spot promptly made for this gentleman. Keeping a firm hold on his bundle, he plunged through a tangle of blackberry bushes that grew beside the road.

The thorny brambles caught at Spot's bundle and held it fast.

"G-r-r-r!" he growled. "I don't want to lose sight of that fat fellow. Unless I'm mistaken, it was Frisky Squirrel. And I've had an eye out for him for a longtime."

After a few frantic tugs he let go of the bundle of clothes and dashed after the squirrel.

It was Frisky Squirrel. He ran up a tree while Spot was struggling in the blackberry thicket. And he scampered from one tree top to another while Spot followed beneath him, barking furiously.

At last Frisky stopped and sat on a limb, to chatter and scold at old dog Spot.

"What are you doing so far from home?" he demanded after a while.

"I've been swimming in the mill pond with the boys," said old dog Spot.

"Then you'd better go back there at once, unless you want a punishing later," Frisky Squirrel told him. "I can hear them whistling for you."

It wasn't far from the mill pond—that place where they were talking, for Spot's chase of Frisky Squirrel had led him back up the hill again. Now Spot cocked his ear in the direction of the pond and listened. Sure enough! he could hear Johnnie Green's whistle.

"I'll see you again," he told Frisky Squirrel.

"Not if I see you first!" Frisky muttered as old Spot started through the woods for the mill pond.

"Come here!" Johnnie Green greeted him sternly when, a few minutes later, he appeared on the bank. "Where are those clothes that you took?"

Spot wagged his tail. He acted very, very friendly. Nobody would have supposed, from his looks, that he had stolen anyone's clothes.

"This is no joke," Johnnie Green declared. "I haven't anything to wear. Get those clothes and bring them back here!"

"I don't know what's the matter with Johnnie," Spot thought. "I didn't touch his things. I don't see why he's so angry."

"Good old Spot!" Johnnie coaxed. "Find the clothes! There's a good fellow!"

He waded toward the bank and snapped his fingers at Spot.

The old dog edged away. Johnnie talked pleasantly enough. But he had a queer look in his eye. Spot thought it safer to keep out of his clutches.

Just then the miller came driving up the hill on a load of corn. When he saw the boys in the pond he stopped his horses.

"Anybody here lost any clothes?" he asked, holding a bundle up in his hand. "I found these by the side of the road. I noticed them hanging on a blackberry bush."

"I'll take 'em!" Johnnie Green cried. "They belong to Red. But you can leave them with me."

The miller tossed the bundle to him.

The boy Red, wearing Johnnie's clothes, was watching everything that went on, from behind a tree. He waited until Johnnie had untied the hard, wet knots in the clothes. Then he stepped out from his hiding place.

"Let's swap!" he said. And while they were swapping, old dog Spot took a swim in the mill pond. Somehow he felt that all was well again.

DROPPING HINTS

On the table in the kitchen of the farmhouse was a leg of mutton. Farmer Green had left it there and gone away. And Mrs. Green had stepped out of the kitchen—nobody knew for how long.

At least old dog Spot and Miss Kitty Cat didn't know. They were left there in the kitchen alone—alone with the leg of mutton.

"Ahem!" said Miss Kitty Cat to old dog Spot. "Don't you think you'd better go and see what's become of Farmer Green?"

She was unusually pleasant, for her. As a rule she had little to say to Spot, except to scold at him.

"I'm comfortable here, thank you," Spot answered. "Farmer Green must be out of sight by this time. So I won't bother to chase after him."

"You could smell out his track, couldn't you?" Miss Kitty Cat suggested.

"Perhaps!" said Spot. "Perhaps! But as I said, I'm comfortable here. I'm going to stay right here in the kitchen." Out of the corner of his eye he looked at Miss Kitty Cat. He could see that she was somewhat displeased by something or other. Her tail was beginning to swell slightly. And that was a sure sign that she was losing her temper. But when she spoke again her voice was as sweet as honey.

"What a beautiful day to go hunting!" she remarked as she sprang into a chair beside the window and looked out. "The woods must be full of birds."

"No doubt!" said Spot dryly. "I went hunting early this morning; and there was plenty of game then."

"Ha!" Miss Kitty exclaimed suddenly. "Do I hear the cows in the cornfield?"

Now, Spot loved to drive the cows out of the corn. But for a wonder, he never even moved an ear.

"I hope the sheep haven't scrambled over the stone wall," Miss Kitty Cat mewed. "If they have, Farmer Green would want you to get them back into the pasture for him."

"Yes!" said Spot with a yawn. "I'm sure he would. And if he needs me he knows where he can find me."

Miss Kitty Cat's tail was growing bigger every moment. And the fur on her back was beginning to stand on end. Still she managed to speak in her very softest voice.

"Did you know—" she inquired—"did you know that Johnnie Green had gone swimming in the mill pond?"

"No!" said Spot. "Has he? I hope he'll have a good time. I had a fine swim yesterday in Black Creek. And I almost caught a muskrat there."

As he spoke he rose and walked across the big, square kitchen and stretched himself out on the floor right in front of the table where the leg of mutton lay.

At that Miss Kitty Cat gave a terrible cry of rage.

"I know why you won't leave the kitchen!" she yowled. "You think I'm going to eat some of that mutton. And that's why you've lain down alongside it."

MRS. GREEN'S MISTAKE

Old dog Spot never moved from the place where he was lying in front of the kitchen table. Although Miss Kitty Cat had told him angrily that he thought she was going to enjoy a luncheon on the leg of mutton that was on the kitchen table, he didn't lose his temper.

"Pardon me!" he said. "You are mistaken. I don't think you're going to have even a taste of this mutton—not while I'm in the kitchen!"

Miss Kitty Cat was furious. She had done her best to make Spot go away. She had dropped a number of hints to get him out of doors. But Spot hadn't taken a single one of them.

"You're a meddlesome old dog," she scolded. "I've a good mind to drag my claws across your nose."

Spot grinned at her.

"If you do," he warned her, "I shall yelp. Then Mrs. Green will hurry back here to see what's going on. And you certainly won't get any mutton while she's in the kitchen. I happen to know that the family's going to have that leg of mutton for dinner to-morrow."

"There ought to be enough of it for everybody," Miss Kitty Cat grumbled. "If I ate a bit of it nobody would ever miss it. And after I've finished my meal there would be nothing to prevent your helping yourself. I certainly shouldn't stand in your way—nor lie in it, either."

Old dog Spot couldn't help sniffing.

"I never snatch any food when Mrs. Green's back is turned," he told Miss Kitty Cat severely. "She feeds me all she thinks I ought to eat. And if I want more, I hunt for it in the woods and fields."

"Don't I hunt?" Miss Kitty Cat hissed. "I keep the house free of rats and mice. Mrs. Green could well spare me a bit of that mutton in return for all I do for her.... I'll thank you, sir, to move away from that table!"

Old Spot began to look somewhat anxious. He had once felt Miss Kitty's sharp claws on his nose. And he didn't care to be scratched by her again. But there was the leg of mutton! He had to guard that for Mrs. Green.

"I wish Mrs. Green would come back," he said to himself. "I don't want a row with this Cat person."

Miss Kitty suddenly spat at him.

Spot knew that that was a danger sign. And he gave a few short, sharp barks.

"There!" he muttered. "That ought to fetch Mrs. Green. If she's in the house she can't help hearing me."

Spot was right. In about a minute Farmer Green's wife came hurrying into the kitchen.

Old dog Spot jumped up and wagged his tail and gave a low-pitched bark as if to say, "I've saved your leg of mutton for you, Mrs. Green."

But she didn't understand him.

"You rascal!" Mrs. Green exclaimed. "You've been teasing the cat again. I can tell by the way she acts. Out you go!" And she opened the door.

Spot went.

XII

RIGHTING A WRONG

Poor Spot! He felt so mournful that he lifted up his muzzle and howled. Farmer Green's wife had just ordered him out of the kitchen. She thought he had been teasing Miss Kitty Cat. And instead he had kept Miss Kitty from tasting the leg of mutton that lay on the kitchen table.

"It's a sad, sad world!" he howled. "I thought Mrs. Green would praise me. But she didn't. She scolded me!"

"Sakes alive!" cried Henrietta Hen as she rushed up to him in the farmyard. "What's the matter with you? Are you trying to bay the moon in the daytime?"

Turkey Proudfoot gobbled at Spot and bade him be still. Turkey Proudfoot was very pompous, for he had an idea that he ruled the farmyard.

Old dog Spot felt so meek, after the scolding that Mrs. Green gave him, that he couldn't find a word to say to anybody that spoke to him.

"I've expected this for some time," the Rooster told Henrietta Hen. "Mrs. Green has put old Spot out of the farmhouse. And Farmer Green intends to put him off the farm. Everyone agrees that he's a nuisance. It's a wonder the folks in the Green family have kept him all these years."

Well, old dog Spot couldn't help hearing what the Rooster said. And he hadn't even heart enough to answer that impertinent boaster.

"Maybe he knows what he's talking about," Spot groaned. "I wish Johnnie Green would come home. He'd stand up for me, if nobody else will."

Then something happened all at once that helped Spot's spirits amazingly. The woodshed door flew open and Miss Kitty Cat all but flew out of it. Farmer Green's wife appeared in the doorway with a broom in her hand. And with it she helped Miss Kitty into the yard. She helped her so much that Miss Kitty never touched the broad stone doorstep at all.

"Scat!" cried Mrs. Green. "I don't want any thieves in my kitchen."

27

It was quite plain that something had displeased Mrs. Green — something in which Miss Kitty Cat had had a part. And old dog Spot thought he knew what that something was.

"Ha!" he barked at Miss Kitty. "So Mrs. Green found you out!" And he ran at Miss Kitty and chased her into a tree. She sat herself down upon a limb and glared at him.

"Wow!" he yelped. "You must have sampled that leg of mutton when you thought Mrs. Green's back was turned. And she must have caught you in the act."

Though that was exactly what had happened, Miss Kitty Cat wouldn't say a word. But she looked whole sentences at him.

Soon Farmer Green's wife came to the door again and called, "Come, Spot! Come, Spot!"

He hurried up to her and caught the piece of meat that she tossed to him.

It was mutton.

XIII

HUNTING

To please old dog Spot Johnnie Green had only to ask him this question, "Want to go hunting, Spot?"

When he heard that, Spot would leave anything he happened to be doing, or give up anything he had intended to do. Perhaps he had expected to dig up and gnaw a choice bone that he had buried somewhere. It might be that he had been planning to chase the cat, or tease Turkey Proudfoot in order to hear him gobble. There wasn't one of those pleasures that Spot wouldn't gladly forgo for the sake of going hunting with Johnnie Green.

When Johnnie Green's father first gave him a shotgun Spot went almost frantic with delight. And they lost no time in starting for the woods. Johnnie Green trudged up the lane with the gun on his shoulder, while Spot ran on ahead of him, returning now and then as if to urge Johnnie to hurry.

They hadn't been long in the woods when Spot suddenly stood still and pointed ahead of him with his nose.

Try as he would, Johnnie couldn't see what Spot was pointing at. So he took a few steps forward until he came abreast of the old dog. Then all at once there was a rumbling whir that sounded to Johnnie Green almost as loud as thunder. A brownish streak flashed from the ground just ahead of him.

He knew that it was a grouse rising. And he fired.

Johnnie Green missed the bird. It had given him such a start that he was still shaking long afterward. He was disappointed, but not less downcast than old Spot.

"Never mind, old boy!" Johnnie said. "We'll have better luck next time!"

But they didn't. Twice more that same thing happened. And after the third miss old Sport turned tail and ran away.

29

"I don't see what's the matter with that boy," he muttered. "I've pointed three birds for him. And he has let every one of them get away.... There's no fun in that kind of shooting."

After that Johnnie couldn't get Spot to go into the woods with him. Whenever Johnnie appeared in the yard with his gun, Spot promptly vanished.

So Johnnie spent a good deal of time shooting at old tin cans which he set on a fence post or a stone wall. And it wasn't long before he found he could hit them at every shot.

At last he came home from the woods one day with a grouse. When he showed it to Spot the old dog actually began teasing him to go hunting.

The next day they set out together for the woods. And Johnnie knocked down the very first grouse that Spot found for him.

Spot brought the bird to Johnnie and laid it proudly at his feet.

"Did Johnnie Green ever give you any of the birds that you find for him?" Miss Kitty Cat inquired when Spot was boasting a bit about the sport he and Johnnie had in the woods. "No!" she said, answering her own question. "You're silly to hunt for him. I prefer to do my hunting alone. Then nobody can take the game away from me."

Old dog Spot walked away from her, to the barn.

"Miss Kitty Cat doesn't know what real hunting is," he told the old horse Ebenezer. "She creeps up on small birds after dark, when they are asleep."

"And you creep up on big birds in the daytime," said old Ebenezer, "so Johnnie Green can shoot them."

Being a sporting dog, Spot couldn't see anything queer in that remark.

"Certainly!" he said.

XIV

MISSING HIS MASTER

Johnnie Green went visiting one summer, after haying was done. Much to old dog Spot's disgust, Johnnie did not take him on this journey. But it was not Spot's fault that he was left at home. Had he not been shut up in the harness room in the barn when Johnnie drove the old horse Ebenezer out of the yard Spot would have followed beneath the buggy.

It was hours before Farmer Green set Spot free. When Farmer Green at last flung open the door of the harness room Spot rushed out and dashed into the road. To his sorrow he couldn't smell a trace of Ebenezer's track. So many other horses had passed by the house since morning that Spot couldn't even tell which way Ebenezer had gone.

In desperation Spot ran up the road a little way. Then he turned around and ran down the hill as far as the gristmill.

By the time he reached the mill pond Spot gave up the chase. He knew it was hopeless.

And seeing several of Johnnie Green's friends swimming in the pond, he joined them.

The boys welcomed him with shouts. And the water was just as cool as ever. But somehow Spot didn't find swimming as pleasant as he always had before. He missed Johnnie Green. There wasn't another boy there that gave Spot the same thrill by whistling to him, or patting him, or romping with him that Johnnie Green gave him.

After a while Spot shook himself and trotted back to Farmer Green's place. He felt homesick. But when he reached the house somehow he felt worse than ever. It was terribly quiet. It was just like a Sunday morning, when everybody was at church. Farmer Green and the hired man were working in the fields. Mrs. Green was busy in the house—too busy to stop and talk with old Spot.

"It's frightfully dull here," Spot groaned. "I wish somebody would shout." And just to break the silence he lifted up his nose and tried to bark.

It was far from a cheerful noise that he made, for he only succeeded in giving a mournful howl. And that sad sound made Spot gloomier than ever.

"Well," he muttered, "there's nothing else to do, so I'll go and dig up that bone that I buried in the orchard last week."

He found the bone where he had hidden it. Yet it did not look half as inviting as it had when he covered it with dirt a few days before. He stared at it dully. Then he put it back in its hole and pawed the dirt over it again.

He found no pleasure in anything. No longer was there any fun in chasing woodchucks. The cows might have stayed in the cornfield all day long and Spot wouldn't have bothered them. He didn't even get any sport out of teasing Miss Kitty Cat.

Strangest of all, he couldn't find any comfort in lying down for a quiet nap. The moment he tried to pass the time away in that fashion he began to think about Johnnie Green and what a nice boy he was. And then he would get up and walk around and around the house. Hour after hour Spot spent in that fashion.

It wasn't many days before he had worn a path in the grass all the way around the farmhouse. When Farmer Green noticed it he didn't scold Spot. He patted his head and said, "Cheer up, old boy! Johnnie'll be back one of these days."

Old dog Spot wagged his tail feebly. But it was hard to wait.

"It wouldn't be so bad," he said to himself, "if there was only somebody to play with. If there was a puppy here on the farm I'd have some one that would be ready to romp whenever I felt like it. And then Johnnie could go away visiting every summer and I wouldn't miss him half as much."

Spot forgot that a puppy wouldn't stay a puppy forever.

XV

A BASKETFUL OF FUN

Johnnie Green came home from his visit at last. The moment Spot heard the old horse Ebenezer come jogging up the road he tore out of the yard and ran, barking, to meet the travellers. He frisked about the buggy, he sprang up and touched Ebenezer's nose with his own, he tried to jump into the buggy beside Johnnie Green.

Spot made such a racket that everybody in the farmhouse knew that Johnnie had returned. The family were just sitting down for dinner. And they all hurried out into the yard. For old dog Spot was not the only one that had missed Johnnie while he was away on his visit.

Johnnie leaped out of the buggy, to be met by a smother of pawings and nosings from old Spot.

"Now, Spot—you behave!" said Johnnie Green. "I'm hungry and I want to get my dinner."

Spot paid not the slightest heed to his young master's objections. "You'll never know how I've missed you," he barked. "And if I want to romp with you for a few minutes, I'm going to; and nobody can stop me."

After a little Spot grew a bit calmer. He let Johnnie Green turn to the buggy and lift out a covered basket.

Spot promptly stuck his nose against it. Then he drew back quickly.

"Wow!" he exclaimed. "This basket smells doggy!"

Spot followed Johnnie into the house. And in the woodshed Johnnie opened the basket and brought out of it a soft, silky, blinking—puppy!

"Wow!" said Spot again. "It was no wonder that I noticed a doggy smell about that basket." And then he said, "G-r-r-r!"

Yes! Spot actually growled at the little newcomer. For the moment he forgot that he had been wishing, for days, that there was a puppy about the place. To tell the truth, he couldn't help feeling the least bit jealous of Johnnie Green's new pet.

In a day or two, however, old Spot liked the puppy as much as anybody else did. He proved to be a playful little chap. And the older he grew the more fun-loving he became.

Sometimes the Puppy Would Bite Spot's Tail.

(Page 73)

There were no more dull days for old dog Spot. When school opened in the fall he no longer moped around the farmhouse, waiting for Johnnie to come home. The puppy kept him too busy to notice Johnnie's absence.

At first Spot found it very pleasant to roll on the ground with his small friend, and pretend to bite him, and upset him off his somewhat wobbly legs. But as time passed Spot began to weary of never-ending play. There were moments when Spot wanted to lie still and doze. But as soon as he had settled himself for a nap the puppy was sure to come bouncing up and sprawl all over him. He would seize one of Spot's long ears between his teeth and give it a bit of a nip. Sometimes he would even pull Spot's tail.

Of course nobody can sleep under such interruptions. Spot learned that when he wanted to rest he had to hide in some place where the puppy couldn't follow him. And as the puppy became bigger Spot found it harder to slip away from him. The youngster would trail Spot into the barn and even as far as the hay-stack in the meadow.

Once the old dog had wished for a puppy. Now, however, he could scarcely wait for this lively youngster to grow into a dog.

A whole year passed before Spot had any peace again. And when another summer had come, and Johnnie Green went visiting again, Spot muttered with a deep groan:

"I hope Johnnie will have sense enough not to bring another puppy with him when he comes home."

XVI

MRS. WOODCHUCK RUNS

Mrs. Woodchuck was on her way home, waddling across the pasture. She had been making a call on Aunt Polly Woodchuck, the herb doctor, who lived under the hill. They had talked over all the news in the neighborhood. And Mrs. Woodchuck had her mind on some gossip that Aunt Polly had told her. Otherwise she might have noticed sooner that old dog Spot had spied her.

If he hadn't spoken he would certainly have caught her that time. For Mrs. Woodchuck was fat and couldn't run as fast as she used to. But when Spot's keen nose caught a scent that told him there was one of the Woodchuck family not far away he just had to give one long-drawn howl.

When Mrs. Woodchuck heard that dreadful sound she scurried for home. She dropped her knitting and the apple that Aunt Polly had given her. And she only managed to pop down the hole that was her front door with Spot scarcely a length behind her.

"Just missed her!" the old dog yelped. "How unlucky!"

"Just escaped!" Mrs. Woodchuck gasped. "How fortunate!"

She knew that she was safe. So she took her own time in crawling through the long hall that led to her one-room dwelling.

"Dear me!" she exclaimed as she entered her underground home and saw that it was empty. "Mr. Woodchuck and Billy are away. I must hurry and warn them that old dog Spot is prowling about the pasture."

Meanwhile Spot lingered at Mrs. Woodchuck's front door. He scratched in the dirt that was thrown up before it. He sniffed at the tracks that the Woodchuck family had made all about.

"I know now where that fat Mrs. Woodchuck lives," he growled. "I'll keep an eye on this hole. Some day I may be able to get between her and her home. And then —"

35

He did not finish what he was saying, but licked his lips as if he had just enjoyed a hearty meal.

For a long time Spot waited there. He could hardly have expected Mrs. Woodchuck to come out and invite him to enter her house. The most that she was likely to do would be to creep not quite to the upper end of her front hall and peer out to see what she could through the small round opening.

"That dame must have a family," Spot thought. "I'd like to meet them — whether there's one youngster or seven. The more the merrier for me."

If Spot had happened to look around just then he would have had his wish granted. Or if the wind had been blowing the other way he could have told, without looking around, that Mrs. Woodchuck's son Billy was gazing at him, with popeyes, from behind a near-by hummock. He had meandered homewards, pausing here and there to nip off a clover head or tear at a plantain leaf, little dreaming that old dog Spot was right in his door-yard.

When he caught sight of the unwelcome caller Billy sat up and took one good, long look at him.

Then Mrs Woodchuck's son turned and ran down the hillside as fast as his short legs would carry him. He didn't stop until he had reached the fence between the pasture and the meadow. Dashing in among the brakes that grew deep along the fence he cowered under the cover that they gave him.

All at once he felt quite ashamed of himself.

"I almost forgot the rule!" he chattered. "The rule says, 'When there's a Dog about, warn everybody!'"

XVII

THE DANGER SIGNAL

Billy Woodchuck remembered, after he had fled from old dog Spot, that he ought to warn his family and his friends. So he sat up, stuck his head out of the tangle of brakes where he had hidden, and gave the danger signal, a sharp whistle.

"Dear me!" he said. "I fear Father and Mother won't hear that. And if they go home they'll run upon old dog Spot. And then there's no knowing what might happen."

He knew that his mother had gone to see Aunt Polly Woodchuck, who lived under the hill. And he knew that his father, with a few cronies, was enjoying a feast in Farmer Green's clover patch.

"I'll hurry over to Aunt Polly's first," he decided, "and tell Mother to beware the Dog."

So Billy Woodchuck scampered off toward the hill where Aunt Polly Woodchuck made her home. When he knocked at Aunt Polly's door and learned that Mrs. Woodchuck had left some time before Billy was much upset.

"Perhaps she went to the clover patch," Aunt Polly suggested. "You know your father sometimes forgets to go home unless somebody goes for him."

Well, Billy started off again. And he hadn't gone far when he heard a sound that made him sit up and listen. Like all his family, he had very sharp ears. And now, after cocking his head on one side for a few moments, he knew that what he heard was old dog Spot grumbling and growling.

"My goodness!" Billy Woodchuck gasped. "He's left our house. And if I don't look out he'll catch me."

At almost the same instant old Spot paused and sniffed the air.

"Ha!" he cried. "I smell a Woodchuck. And if I'm not mistaken it's a different Woodchuck from the one I chased a little while ago."

Billy Woodchuck and Spot began to run at the same time. Billy headed for home; and Spot headed for him.

Again old dog Spot was just a bit too late. Billy Woodchuck darted into the hole in the hillside not a second too soon. He could hear Spot panting close behind him.

"Such luck!" Spot growled. "There's another that's got away from me. There's the second one that I've run into that hole. I suppose they're chuckling inside their house and making all manner of fun of me."

The old dog was mistaken. Billy Woodchuck was not chuckling. He found nobody at home. It was plain that his parents were still abroad.

"They may be coming from the clover patch now," he groaned. And if they are, they're sure to stumble upon that terrible creature at the door. I must warn them before it's too late."

While Spot was still snorting and snuffling around the Woodchuck family's front door, Billy Woodchuck crept out of the back door and started for the clover patch. Little did he know that his mother had already stolen out the same way, to warn him and his father.

When unwelcome callers come, a back door is sometimes a convenient thing to have about a house.

XVIII

A CROWDED HOUSE

Old dog Spot never once guessed that there was a back door to the Woodchuck family's home in the pasture. He had chased Mrs. Woodchuck into her house. He had likewise hunted her son Billy into the same front door through which his mother had scrambled only a short time before.

"There must be more of these fat folks about the pasture," Spot thought. "I'll range around a bit and see if I can't surprise another."

So he began running about the pasture in big circles. And he was lucky enough, before long, to come upon Mr. Woodchuck himself, who had dined so heartily on clover heads that he had decided to go to his chamber and take a nap.

Spot was unlucky enough to lose him. Mr. Woodchuck had been feeling quite sleepy. But when he suddenly found himself pursued by a dog he was wide awake in an instant and running like a youngster.

He reached his home just in time.

"Well, that makes the third one that's inside the house," Spot muttered, shortly afterward, as he paused to get his breath.

Little did he know how mistaken he was. There wasn't even one of the Woodchuck family at home; for Mr. Woodchuck had at once hurried out the back way, because he wanted to find his wife and his son and tell them to keep away from old dog Spot.

Soon Spot took a few more turns around the pasture. And this time he ran across Mrs. Woodchuck again.

He had no sooner run her to earth once more than he found Billy for the second time.

"This is a twin brother of the fellow I chased home once before," Spot panted, little dreaming that Billy Woodchuck had come back into the daylight.

"This twin is just as spry as the other one was," Spot gasped as he reached for Billy right at his door—and missed him.

After that the old dog chased Mr. Woodchuck, then his wife, and next their son Billy Woodchuck. And he didn't succeed in catching any one of the three. Each of them beat him in the race to the Woodchuck family's front door.

Old Spot began to feel quite upset.

"I don't see what the matter with me to-day," he puzzled. "I hope I'm not getting so old that I'm weeble." (By that he meant weak and feeble.)

"This last one makes eight that I've followed all the way to this door," Spot growled. "There can't be many more left in the pasture. I'm going to lie down behind this hummock and wait till they come out."

So he hid a little way off and watched closely.

He had been there a long time when Mr. Crow at last flew low over the pasture and alighted in a tree near-by.

"What are you waiting for?" he asked Spot.

"Woodchucks!" said Spot. "This burrow is full of them."

"Are you sure?" Mr. Crow inquired.

"I chased eight of them home," Spot explained.

"That's odd," said Mr. Crow. "There have been only three living here lately. And they don't live here any more."

"They don't!" Spot cried.

"No!" Mr. Crow told him. "They moved this afternoon."

Old dog Spot sprang to his feet.

"Where did they go?" he demanded.

"Ah!" Mr. Crow croaked. "That's telling." And he would say no more.

Then Spot went back to the farmyard.

Meanwhile the Woodchuck family were working hard, digging a new home for themselves at the other end of the pasture. They had all met at last on the edge of the clover patch. And Mr. Woodchuck had declared that they must move at once, because it wasn't safe to live in their old house any longer. He said that old dog Spot would be sure to keep an eye on it for some time.

They soon found a place that suited them all very well.

"We'll live here," said Mr. Woodchuck to his wife and their son Billy. "You two can take turns digging while I sit up and watch for old dog Spot. After all the running I did to-day it wouldn't be safe for me to do any digging."

That was Mr. Woodchuck's plan. And they followed it.

XIX

OFF FOR THE CIRCUS

Great circus posters had covered one side of Farmer Green's barn for weeks. Ever since some men came and pasted them on the barn Johnnie Green had studied them carefully. He had practiced bareback riding on his pony, Twinkleheels. He had tried a high dive into the mill pond from the top of the dam. And much to old dog Spot's disgust Johnnie had tried to make him jump through a hoop covered with paper.

Spot had refused flatly to do anything of the kind. If he had known that his young master had half a notion to teach him to jump through a hoop of fire Spot would have run away — at least until circus time had come and gone.

"What puts all these queer ideas into Johnnie's head?" the old dog asked his friend Ebenezer, the horse, one day.

"Don't you know?" said Ebenezer. "It's those circus pictures. Johnnie won't think of anything else until the twenty-third of August."

"What's going to happen then?" Spot inquired.

"That's the day when the circus comes to the village," the old horse explained. "The whole family's going to see it."

"Do you expect to take them?"

"No!" Ebenezer replied. "Farmer Green will hitch the bays to the carryall. And to tell the truth, I'll be just as pleased to stay behind. It will be a great day to take naps here at home."

"It will be a lonesome day, with everybody away," said Spot. "I believe I'll go to the circus myself."

"Farmer Green may decide to leave you here," the old horse suggested.

"Then I'll surprise him," said Spot. "I'll hide behind a tree until Farmer Green has driven out of the yard. And then I'll follow the carryall."

The old dog began to tell everybody in the farmyard that he was going to the circus on the twenty-third of August. Of course some of the farmyard folk were jealous of him. The Rooster remarked that he didn't believe Spot would hear any crowing at the circus that would be worth listening to. Turkey Proudfoot said that when it came to strutting the circus couldn't show Spot any that couldn't be beaten right there on the farm. And Henrietta Hen, who went to the county fair the year before, declared that she shouldn't care to go to the village except to see a poultry show.

But old dog Spot didn't mind anything they said. And when the twenty-third of August came he lingered about the farmyard. Early in the morning he saw Farmer Green run the carryall into the yard and harness the bays to it. Then the rest of the family came out of the house.

Spot, from his hiding place behind a tree, was pleased to see that Johnnie Green did not forget to bring a big lunch basket with him.

At last everybody was ready to start. And then, to Spot's dismay, Farmer Green caught sight of his nose, sticking out from behind a tree.

"That dog means to follow us," he cried. "I'll have to shut him up in the barn." And to old Spot he called, "Come here, sir!"

Spot didn't dare disobey. With his tail between his legs he crept up to the carryall. And though he whined and begged to be taken to the circus, Farmer Green caught hold of his collar and led him into the barn. Then Farmer Green closed the door.

Poor Spot had to give one loud howl when he heard the wheels of the carryall crunching on the gravel driveway.

XX

SPOT GOES TO TOWN

The bays had to step lively that morning, for Farmer Green's family didn't want to be late for the circus parade in the village.

There were many other teams on the road, and almost nobody to be seen working in the fields. It seemed to Johnnie Green as if everybody had made up his mind to go to the circus. The only thing that troubled him was that his father didn't drive fast enough to suit him.

Half way from the farm to the village Farmer Green stopped the bays at a watering trough. Johnnie jumped out of the carryall to uncheck them, so they could drink. And there, beneath the carriage, was old dog Spot!

"Spot's followed us!" Johnnie Green cried.

The old dog whisked out from between the wheels and frolicked about Johnnie. He didn't act at all guilty.

"Well, I never!" said Farmer Green. "I certainly shut the barn door after I shoved him inside."

Spot gave a few short, sharp barks, as if to say, "Yes! But you forgot the window that was open."

He had scrambled through the window and overtaken the carryall before it reached the gristmill.

Well, what could Farmer Green do? They had come too far to send Spot back home.

"We'll have to take him with us now," said Johnnie Green's father, "though he'll be a nuisance because the village will be crowded to-day."

As soon as the bays had had their drink the party started on again. And old dog Spot was content. He did not mind the dust that the bays' heels kicked up as he followed beneath the carriage. And the faster they trotted, the more they pleased him; for he was as anxious as Johnnie Green to get to town and see the crowds and the fun.

Once a surly dog ran out from a farmhouse and tried to reach him. That made Spot somewhat uneasy.

"I don't want to stop to fight this fellow," he thought. "If I do, I'll be left behind."

Luckily Farmer Green cut at the strange dog with his whip and bade him be off.

Spot grinned as he sneaked away, yelping.

At last they entered the village. Main Street was thronged with people. Carriages and wagons of all sorts lined the road on both sides — glistening buggies with red ribbons tied in bows about the whip stocks, old lumber wagons with chairs set behind the driver's seat.

Johnnie Green had never seen such a gathering — not even at the fair.

"The whole county's here!" he exclaimed. "I hope we'll find a good place to stop, where we can see the parade."

They did. Farmer Green backed the bays into the last open space in the gutter. And Johnnie Green was greatly relieved.

The crowd made such a roar, with its talking and laughter, that old Spot cowered down under the carryall and almost wished he had stayed at home. The cries of men selling peanuts and popcorn, squawkers and toy balloons, mingled with the shouts of small boys and the squeals of their sisters.

"Goodness!" Spot murmured. "What a racket! It hurts my ears."

A moment later he stuck his nose out from beneath the carriage and burst into a mournful howl.

"Keep still!" Farmer Green ordered.

Little did he know, then, what made Spot cry like that. But in a minute or two Johnnie Green heard the same thing that Spot's sharp ears had caught first. And Johnnie howled too.

"Hear the band!" he shouted. "Hurrah! The parade's coming!"

XXI

THE CIRCUS PARADE

The crash and blare of the circus band came nearer and nearer. Johnnie Green craned his neck out of the carryall, as it stood at the side of Main Street, and tried to get a glimpse of the parade.

Old dog Spot did not howl again, but stole out beside the bays and looked up the street too.

Soon a man with a tall, shiny hat on his head rode a proud, prancing horse around a corner. And behind him six more horses with gay plumes on their bridles made a wide turn as they swung into view. On top of the high red wagon that they drew sat the band, all in red suits and playing away like mad.

Spot couldn't help whining. Although the bandsmen were playing the liveliest air they knew, music always made Spot sad. And he was glad when the band wagon had passed on.

Other wagons, blazoned with red and gold, followed.

Old dog Spot's hair began to rise along his back and he sniffed, growling. He had noticed a strange mixture of the queerest odors. He didn't know, for a moment, whether to run away or not.

"Oh, see the tiger!" Johnnie Green shouted. "And the lions! And the monkeys! And the bear!"

"See them!" Spot yelped. "I say, smell them!"

He felt better when the animals in their cages had gone creaking past. And he forgot his uneasiness as he watched dozens of horses, ridden by folk whose bespangled clothes glittered in the sunlight.

Then came a funny man in a little, two-wheeled cart, driving a donkey. This was the clown. He bowed and smiled to everybody, right and left, and even threw kisses at some of the girls. His painted face, his bag-like clothes, and his odd little round, pointed hat made Johnnie Green laugh. And to Johnnie's great delight, when the clown saw Spot he whistled.

Old Spot was all for dashing out into the street. But Farmer Green wouldn't let him do that. Spot had to be content with barking at the clown.

Then a man on a brisk little horse came down the street. He had a big voice. And he kept using it all the time, shouting so everybody would be sure to hear, "Look out for your bosses! The elephants are coming!"

And they came. The elephants came. When Spot saw their huge forms plodding down Main Street he dived beneath the carryall again and shivered until the last one had passed along.

The bays stirred restlessly as the elephants neared them. And the younger of the pair snorted with fear.

Farmer Green talked to them in a soothing voice and told them there wasn't any danger. But nobody thought of talking to old dog Spot. Every one forgot about him. And he was just as badly frightened as the bays, especially when a terrible tooting and screeching burst forth.

Spot jumped almost out of his skin.

"Sakes alive!" he howled. "What awful voices the elephants have!"

"The steam calliope!" Johnnie Green cried. "And that's the end of the parade."

XXII

THE CIRCUS GROUNDS

The Green family ate their luncheon in the carryall on Main Street, after the circus parade had passed. They didn't forget to give old dog Spot something to eat out of the big basket that they had brought with them from home. Although they hadn't expected him to go to the village with them, there was more than enough food for everybody. Even Johnnie Green's appetite wasn't equal to all the goodies that his mother had provided.

People were already starting for the circus grounds on the outskirts of the village. Johnnie Green noticed them uneasily.

"We don't want to be late for the show," he reminded his father.

"We'll get there in time," Farmer Green assured him.

And they did. Soon they followed the crowd through the village streets until they came in sight of the "big top," the great tent with flags flying above it, and smaller tents all around.

Farmer Green turned the bays into a yard near-by, where he unharnessed and fed them. Then he tied one end of a rope to Spot's collar and fastened the other end to a carriage wheel.

"There!" he said. "Now we're ready."

Old dog Spot didn't want to be left behind. He tugged at the rope and whined.

"Be quiet!" Johnnie Green's father said to him. "You followed us to the village. And now you'll have to behave yourself. They wouldn't let you into the show."

Then the Green family turned their backs on him.

"They needn't think they can keep me here," Spot growled. "I didn't run all the way from the farm to the village to be tied to a wagon wheel."

Johnnie Green and his father and mother hadn't been gone a quarter of an hour when Spot succeeded in slipping his collar over his head. Then he dashed out of the yard and ran to the circus grounds as fast as he could go.

Spot mingled with the crowds of people that were pouring into the big tent. He worked his way in and out among the throng, all but tripping many of the pleasure seekers.

Though he looked everywhere, he couldn't find the Green family. They had already passed through the entrance and were enjoying the sights inside the canvas.

At last Spot met a man—a circus man—who was very friendly. It was pleasant to get a kind word from somebody, after so many people had told him to "get out," and had given him a shove.

This kindly person called Spot into a low tent and patted him. He gave Spot a bit of meat and even thought to offer him a drink of water.

"This is a fine pointer," the man remarked to a friend of his who was with him. "He hasn't any collar; so he must be anybody's dog. And he might as well be mine."

Spot wagged his tail. He didn't quite understand what his new acquaintance was saying. But it seemed to be something nice.

And then Spot decided, suddenly, that he had stayed in that tent long enough. For the pleasant man found a piece of rope and tried to tie it about Spot's neck.

"I've been tied up once to-day; and once is enough," Spot growled. Slipping out of the man's grasp, Spot ran out of doors.

Both men followed him. For a few minutes they chased him. One of them tripped over a guy rope and sprawled on the ground. And to escape the other Spot dodged under a canvas wall where it lifted slightly at the bottom.

He found himself in a huge tent where hundreds of people sat all around on tiers of seats. Men and horses were capering about in the center of the place. And somewhere a band was playing.

He was under the big top.

XXIII

SPOT SEES THE SHOW

Old dog Spot was bewildered. When he crawled under the canvas he had not dreamed that he was entering the main tent of the circus. He saw so many strange sights that he didn't know whether to bark or to crawl away and hide somewhere. Yet among all those people he felt lonely. He couldn't see anybody he knew.

All at once the bandsmen began to play louder than ever. They seemed to be trying to burst their horns — or themselves. And men in flowing robes, each one standing in a sort of little two-wheeled cart and driving four horses abreast, came tearing past the place where Spot was standing.

It was a race! And if there was one thing that Spot liked more than another it was a race of any kind. He gave a few delighted barks and ran after the galloping horses.

Spot followed them twice around the big tent. And just as he fell into a jog — for the race was finished — he heard a whistle that gave him a great thrill. He stood still for an instant. Then he dashed toward the nearest seats.

A moment later he was fawning upon Johnnie Green, who sat in the lowest row and seemed as glad to see Spot as Spot was to see him.

Lying between Johnnie's feet, Spot watched the rest of the show.

At last the circus was over. The Green family, with Spot at their heels, went back to the place where they had left the bays and the carryall. And in a few minutes more they were on their way back to Pleasant Valley and home.

That morning everybody on the road had seemed to be in a great hurry to get to the village. And now, late in the afternoon, everybody was in just as great a hurry to get away from it. Farmer Green kept the bays at a spanking trot, only pausing to let them breathe now and then on the hills.

Spot, however, was not in such haste that he didn't stop and give a good trouncing to the dog that had rushed out at him earlier in the day. Spot sent the surly fellow yelping into his master's yard. Then he rushed down the road to overtake the carryall.

But, to everybody's surprise, when they reached home old dog Spot was missing.

"He'll come back," Farmer Green said. "Probably he's stopped somewhere to chase a rabbit or something. He'll be along after a while."

But after the cows were milked old Spot was still absent. And after the family had eaten supper he had failed to appear. Bedtime came. Still no Spot!

Johnnie Green felt very sad when he went upstairs.

He felt even worse when morning came. He had hoped that Spot would be in the yard, begging for his breakfast.

Johnnie Green was able to eat only a little of his own breakfast. And as soon as he left the table he went to the barn and harnessed his pony, Twinkleheels, to the little buggy with the red wheels.

Then Johnnie started for the village.

XXIV

HOME AGAIN

Johnnie Green drove his pony, Twinkleheels, back over the road that led to the village. Now and then he stopped at a farmhouse to inquire whether anybody had seen old dog Spot, who had vanished on the way home from the circus the evening before.

Nobody had set eyes on him. And Johnnie Green drove on and on, feeling more and more miserable all the while.

At last, as he turned a sharp bend of the road, he heard a bark. There was no mistaking it. It was Spot's.

There was a joyful meeting then. Johnnie sprang out of the buggy and Spot sprang into his arms. And Johnnie hugged the old fellow tightly, right there in the middle of the road.

"What in the world has kept you here ever since yesterday?" Johnnie asked.

Spot must have understood. Anyhow, he dashed to one side of the road. And, following him, Johnnie found there a robe that belonged to his father. It had dropped out of the carryall the evening before, when the Green family were on their way home from seeing the circus. Nobody in the carriage had missed it. But old Spot, running under the carriage, had seen it fall. And he had stayed behind to guard it all through the long night.

Of course Spot couldn't tell Johnnie Green all this. But Johnnie wasn't slow in guessing what had happened.

He picked up the robe and put it under the seat of the little buggy. Then he and Spot both jumped in. And Johnnie turned Twinkleheels' head toward home.

Back at the farm almost everybody said that old dog Spot was a hero. Farmer Green exclaimed that Spot was a faithful old fellow. And Mrs. Green set out such a meal for him as Spot had never seen before in all his life.

Now, there were two or three of Spot's neighbors in the farmyard that didn't like the praise he was getting. Turkey Proudfoot, the gobbler, remarked that if people didn't know enough to come home to roost at night he saw no reason for making a fuss about it. Miss Kitty Cat declared that so far as she was concerned she would have been just as well pleased if Spot hadn't come back to the farm at all. And Henrietta Hen had more to say than anyone else. She hurried up to old dog Spot himself and insisted on talking with him.

"Huh!" she exclaimed. "You only spent one day at the circus, while last fall I stayed a whole week at the county fair."

"Did you hear a band at the fair?" Spot asked her.

"Yes!"

"Did you see any races?"

"There were races every day; but I didn't care to watch them," Henrietta Hen answered.

"Did you see any elephants at the fair?" Spot demanded.

"Elephants?" said Henrietta Hen. "What are elephants?"

Spot pointed — with his nose — to one of the posters on the barn.

"There's a picture of some elephants," he told her. "And I must say it's a good one."

"There were no elephants at the county fair," Henrietta Hen admitted as she gazed at the circus poster on the side of the barn. "Why, every one of them has two tails!" she cried. "I don't see how they know whether they're going backward or forward."

"Maybe they don't know," Spot retorted. "Maybe that's part of the fun in being an elephant. For I suppose there's fun of some sort in being anybody, even a-a-a — "

"Even a what?" Henrietta snapped. "Were you going to say a Hen?"

"I was," Spot replied. "But I remembered that it wouldn't be polite."

"I should say not!" Henrietta Hen cackled. "I should say not!" And then, being very angry, she hurried off to tell the rooster what had happened.

"I'll have to be careful how I talk to these farmyard folks," Spot muttered. "They haven't had a chance to learn some of the things that I know.

"For I've been to the village and seen the world—and the circus, too," added old dog Spot.

THE END

Milton Keynes UK
Ingram Content Group UK Ltd.
UKHW040902181023
430840UK00004B/163